THE FIREFIGHTERS

WRITTEN BY **Sue Whiting**   PICTURES BY **Donna Rawlins**

WALKER BOOKS
AND SUBSIDIARIES

BRIIIIIING! BRIIIIIING!

The alarm screams.

'Quick!' I say. 'Coats and boots!'

'Hats, too,' says Mia.

'Hurry, Mrs Iverson,' says Jack.

'There's a fire!'

We're being firefighters — just like the **REAL** ones.

'Climb on board,' I say.

'Squash in, Mrs Iverson,' says Mia.

'The door won't close.'

'Siren's on,' says Jack. 'Let's go, go, go!'

We're in our fire engines.

They're just like the **REAL** ones.

EEE-ORR! EEE-ORR! EEE-ORR!

The siren yells.

'Quick!' I say. 'Round the corner.'

'And up the hill,' says Mia.

'Then into Drury Lane,' says Mrs Iverson.

'No!' shouts Jack. 'That's the wrong way.'

Silly Mrs Iverson.

We scream out the door.

EEE-ORR! EEE-ORR! EEE-ORR!

We tear past the climbing fort and hidey tunnel.

We flash past the sandpit.

EEE-ORR! EEE-ORR! EEE-ORR!

Everyone stops and stares. We don't have time to wave.

Our fire engines are fast and noisy — just like the **REAL** ones.

'There's the fire,' I say. 'Quick! Pull over.'

'Connect the hoses,' says Mia.

'We have to hurry,' says Mrs Iverson,

'or Lulu's Ice-Creamery will go up too!'

'This could get dangerous,'

says Jack. 'We must be careful.'

The fire is hot. The flames crack and
pop and tickle the sky.

The smoke is really stinky.

'Oxygen masks,' says Mrs Iverson.

Good thinking. We pull on our masks.

Mia and Jack hold one hose.

Mrs Iverson and I hold the other.

Water shoots out and blasts the fire.

whoosh! whoosh!

whoosh!

We're firefighters, brave and strong — just like the **REAL** ones.

'Fire's out,' I say.

'We did it!' says Mia.

'And we saved Lulu's,'
says Mrs Iverson.

'Good job, everyone,'
says Jack.

We flop to the ground — tired and dirty.

Then ... **EEE-ORR! EEE-ORR! EEE-ORR!** What's that?

EEE-ORR! EEE-ORR! EEE-ORR! A siren?

'Look!' I say.

'Wow,' says Mia.

'Too noisy,' yells Jack,
covering his ears.

'Surprise!' says Mrs Iverson.

'Now move back.'

It's a fire engine. **A REAL ONE.**

The fire engine drives into the yard

and stops right outside our classroom.

The doors swing open
and out step two firefighters.
REAL LIVE ONES!

Mrs Iverson gets us to sit in the shade.

The firefighters tell us stories about fighting fires

and rescuing people from burning buildings.

It sounds exciting — and scary.

They tell us if there is a fire in a building we're in,

we should get down low and ***GO, GO, GO!***

'Let's pretend,'
says one of the firefighters.

'Oh no!' shouts the other.
'There's smoke!
There must be a fire.'

We're not silly.
We know what to do.
We get down low and
take off like mad!

'We're good at pretending,'
I tell the firefighters.
'We can see that!'
they say.

When we are sitting down again,
one of the firefighters says,
'Would anyone like
to climb on board?'

'YES!' we all shout.
And we do.
Three at a time.

The fire engine is big and red and shiny.

There are dials and buttons everywhere.

Mia and I take turns at switching on the siren.

Jack speaks into the radio.

'Don't worry. We're on our way,' he says.

I love it.

I **REALLY** do.

'You know, we're firefighters too,'
I tell the firefighters.
'Just not **REAL** ones
like you ...
YET!'

For Samantha, Hayden and
all the crazy cats in 1/2 Red,
even Ms P
SW

For Mia
and thanks to Henry Callum
for the fire engine drawing
DR

First published 2008 by Walker Books Ltd
87 Vauxhall Walk, London SE11 5HJ

This edition published 2011

10 9 8 7 6 5 4 3 2 1

Text © 2008 Sue Whiting
Illustrations © 2008 Donna Rawlins

This book has been typeset in Abadi and Machine

Printed in Singapore

British Library Cataloguing in Publication Data:
a catalogue record for this book is available from the British Library

ISBN 978-1-4063-2999-5

www.walker.co.uk